Adapted by Kitty Richards
Based on the series created by Dan Povenmire & Jeff "Swampy" Marsh

D0037298

DISNEY
XD

DISNEP PRESS
New York

Printed in the United States of America
First Edition
10 9 8 7 6 5 4 3 2 1

Library of Congress Catalog Card Number on file.
ISBN 978-1-4231-1799-5

For more Disney Press fun, visit www.disneybooks.com.
Visit DisneyChannel.com

Part One

Chapter 1

Candace sat in her pink bedroom, holding a banana to her ear, as she pretended to call her not-so-secret crush, Jeremy Johnson. "Hello," she began. "Is this the Johnson residence? I'd like to speak to Jeremy Johnson." She smiled. "This is Candace Flynn. Why am I calling, you ask?" She referred to her open notebook, which listed several "reasons for calling." She chose one. ". . . Because I have a question

about our algebra assignment. Thank you, I'll hold." She frantically flipped through her notebook. "Okay, okay. Let's see . . . opening jokes, opening jokes . . . Hey-ah, Jeremy. This is Candace Flynn. So, what do you get when you cross a yak and a Martian?"

Just then, the bedroom door opened with a squeak. "Honey," said a voice, "could I interrupt for just a sec?"

"Why, Jeremy Johnson," Candace said in a teasing tone, "did you just call me honey?" Suddenly her eyes widened in surprise and she turned bright red. She realized that her mom was standing in her doorway!

"No, Candace," her mother answered. "I just wanted to tell you I'm off to my book club. I left a phone number on the fridge in case of an emergency. And, Candace, honey?"

"Yes, Mom?" she asked.

"I hope you're not planning on talking to that banana all afternoon," her mom said with a smile as she headed out the door.

Outside in the backyard, Candace's brother, Phineas, stood beneath a tree, wearing a sombrero on his head and holding a pointer

in his hand. He addressed the "crowd," which consisted only of Perry the Platypus, the family pet. "Ladies and platypuses, introducing the latest party craze to sweep the nation: The Amazing Mariachi Tree!" As spirited music began to play, Phineas pointed to the large tree, which had seven mariachi players sitting in its branches. His stepbrother, Ferb, who was playing the trumpet above them, leaned back and lost his balance, falling out of the

tree! The other mariachi players followed, groaning in pain as they landed. As Ferb

popped up from the ground, a sombrero fell right onto his head.

Phineas winced. "I think the lesson here is: Don't drink too much chocolate milk before

planning the day's activity," he concluded.

It was time for the band to go home. Phineas and Ferb waved goodbye to the musicians. "Bye, guys!" called Phineas. "Sorry. Good work there, though. There's that smile, Arturo. *Gracias.*"

Just then, Phineas and Ferb's friend Isabella came walking up to them. She was wearing a

pink jumper with a matching bow in her hair. She had a really big crush on Phineas, but he had no idea. "Hi, Phineas," she said sweetly.

"Oh, hi, Isabella," Phineas replied.

Isabella smiled. "Whatcha do—" she began to say, then hiccupped loudly. Embarrassed, she put both her hands to her mouth.

"Are you okay?" Phineas asked, concerned.

"Yeah," Isabella said. "I just came by to see whatcha do—" She hiccupped again. "—ing."

"Wow," commented Phineas. "That's a bad case of the hiccups you got there."

"I know," Isabella said with a sigh. "They're driving me crazy!" She hiccupped once more.

"Not to fear, Isabella," Phineas told her. "Ferb and I will help cure your hiccups!"

Isabella hiccupped in response.

Just then Phineas noticed something. "Hey, where's Perry?" he asked.

Perry the Platypus was sneaking off to a row of garbage cans. He quickly pulled out his fedora and placed it on his head. It was time to transform himself, from his secret identity as a mere house pet into the amazing Agent P! He took the lid off one of the cans and hopped inside. Oops, wrong can. He hopped back out, removed a banana peel from his head, and hopped inside the next can. A hidden slide whisked him directly to the controls of Platypus Cave, his secret hide-out. He landed in front of

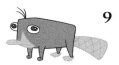

a huge video screen, as garbage poured down on him.

Just then, Major Monogram, Perry's superior officer, appeared on the screen. The major gave Perry the information about his latest mission. "Good morning, Agent P," he said. "Dr. Doofenshmirtz is on the move. We tracked him to these coordinates when we suddenly lost his signal." At that moment, the major's face was replaced by a map with a big, red X marking the spot.

The major continued. "We have two scenarios to explain his disappearance. First,

magical elves caused Dr. Doofenshmirtz to vanish to the land of angry corn people. The second is that he may be on a secret hideout-shaped island with his initial, *D*, carved into it. Satellites found it in the . . . exact . . . spot . . . where . . . he . . . vanished." The major suddenly realized how silly the first scenario sounded. "Uh . . . you know what? Uh, forget the magical elves thing. Way off base with that. Anyway, on your way, Agent P."

Perry took off immediately, jumping into a white convertible. Flames shot out of the sides of the car as it blasted off into the air.

In the backyard, Phineas was still trying to help Isabella get rid of her hiccups. "Okay, Isabella," he began, "the best way to cure hiccups is to scare them away." He pointed

at her. "So, what scares you?" he asked.

"Hmm," began Isabella, putting her hand to her chin and thinking hard. She hiccupped. "Well, there was this haunted house at the state fair"—she hiccupped again—"that was pretty scary."

Phineas's eyes lit up. "That's it!" he cried. "Ferb and I are going to make you the scariest haunted house ever! With zombies!" He made

a snarling face. "And werewolves! And ghosts and vampires!" he exclaimed, pretending to cover his face with a cape. "And witches!"

Little did they know that Candace was standing right behind them. She cleared her throat.

Phineas turned around. "Oh, hey, Candace," he said.

"Phineas!" Candace shouted, putting her hands on her hips. "The only way you're building a haunted house in this backyard is over my dead body!"

"That's the idea," replied Phineas, trying to sound like Count Dracula.

Candace scowled. "That's it, you little psycho! I'm calling Mom." She ran off into the house and slammed the door behind her. Then she suddenly opened it again.

"And I am *not* using the banana this time!" she yelled. She slammed the door again.

Phineas looked at Ferb and Isabella in disbelief. "You guys heard that, right? It wasn't

just me?" Ferb and Isabella just shrugged.

Inside the house, Candace was fuming. Build a haunted house, my foot, she thought angrily. She grabbed the number that her mother had left, picked up the phone, and began to dial. They're *so* busted! she thought.

"Yes, hello," said Candace in a super-proper voice when someone picked up the phone. "This is an emergency. I'd like to speak with Linda Flynn. To whom am I presently speaking?"

"Uh, Jeremy, that's whom," a male voice responded.

Candace's eyes widened. She looked down at the paper in her hand. It read: BOOK CLUB JOHNSON'S 555-0105. Johnson's? It couldn't be!

"J-J-Jeremy?" she stammered. "J-J-Jer-Jeremy who?"

"Jeremy Johnson," he replied. "My mom's hosting a book club today. Who's this?" he asked curiously.

Candace quickly held the paper close to the receiver and crumpled it up so it sounded like static. "We seem to be breaking up," she said. Then she frantically tried to come up with other excuses. "I-I'm going into a tunnel . . ." she fibbed. "Sunspots . . ." she added. "I . . . No *hablo español!*" Mortified, she hung up the phone and put her hands to her mouth. Could her day get any worse?

Chapter 2

High over Dr. Doofenshmirtz's secret island, Perry parachuted from an airplane. As he plummeted through the air, two wings that looked a lot like platy-pus tails opened up. He flapped them and guided himself to the roof of the island. He took off his helmet,

adjusted his fedora, then opened the roof hatch and lowered himself down on a rope. Inside, he found a circular room with windows

all around it. He pressed himself against a wooden crate, his arms outstretched, thinking he was safe. Just then, metal cuffs slid down over his wrists, around his feet and even on his tail! He was trapped!

Dr. Doofenshmirtz smirked. "Perry the Platypus? *Here?* How could this be? I'm shocked," he said, pretending to be surprised. He used a pointer to indicate a series of posters with pictures of every move Perry had made. "I mean, it would have taken a total evil mastermind to have guessed that you'd track me to this point, find the secret hideout, glide in under the radar, infiltrate this access vent, and make your way over to this crate, activating my automatic arm and leg restraints. . . ."

He pointed to another poster. "Oh, right here, this is the part where I get all sarcastic and pretend you surprised me." He put his hand to his mouth in pretend shock. "Oh, Perry the Platypus! How? What the—? Who the—? Why the—? Ohh! Finally ending here when I finish showing you my brilliant plan."

He smiled and continued. "You see, Perry the Platypus, this secret hideout doesn't actually belong to me. It belonged to my mentor, Professor Destructicon!" He bent the pointer, and it sprang out of his hands, breaking something with a loud crash. "Sadly, he was just captured in the midst of his latest plan: to set fire to the sun!" Dr. Doofenshmirtz exclaimed loudly. "Redundant, perhaps, but before they locked him away, Kevin asked a favor of me. To prevent them from discovering his hidden lair and all its secrets, would I please set fire to the sun? And I was, like, 'Dude, you really got to let that one go. It's—it's a ball of fire. It makes no sense!'"

Dr. Doofenshmirtz walked back over to Perry. "So he asked me to simply destroy his hideout instead, which I will now do using my new Disintevaporator!" With a flourish, he swept away a sheet to reveal a small purple box with controls on it. He cleared his throat. "And you, Perry the Platypus, will now be disintevaporated along with it!" He cackled with glee. Finally, one of his evil plans was actually going to work!

Meanwhile, Candace was trying to psych herself up to call Jeremy back. She picked up

the phone. "Okay, just breathe and relax," she said to herself. She exhaled. "Let's try this again. Hi! Uh, Linda Flynn, please. But, if she's too busy, uh, then maybe there's someone else who can deliver a message to her? Maybe someone in their teens?" she added.

"Uh, who is this?" a little girl's voice answered.

"This is Candace, Candace Flynn," she said nervously. "And who is this?"

"I'm Suzy, Jeremy's little sister," the girl replied.

"Well, it is such a pleasure to meet you on the—" Candace started to say.

"You called for Jeremy, didn't you?" Suzy interrupted.

Candace's eyes flew open. "Jeremy? Um, no, no, no, no, no!" she stammered.

Even though Suzy was young, she was used to girls calling for her older brother. She knew

all of their tricks. "You say you want your mom, but you really want Jeremy. Isn't that right?"

Candace gulped. "That's not true!"

"I'm sorry," Suzy said. She crumpled up a piece of paper into the receiver. "We seem to be breaking up."

"Stop crinkling paper!" Candace cried. "I know that trick!"

"Bye-bye," Suzy said.

"Wait, wait, wait!" Candace exclaimed. She took a deep breath. "It's true," she confessed. "I want to speak to Jeremy."

"I thought so," Suzy said. "Jeremy, some girl's on the phone for you!" she called out sweetly. Then her voice became very serious. "But never, ever forget," she told Candace, "I am and always *will* be Jeremy's favorite girl. Got it?"

"Mm-mm," Candace replied nervously, nodding her head. "Yes."

Jeremy picked up the phone. "I got it, my

favorite girl," he said to Suzy. "Jeremy here," he said into the receiver.

Candace gasped. "Jeremy!"

"Candace?" Jeremy asked.

"Uh . . . yeah, yeah, it's me," replied Candace. She laughed nervously.

"Hey, you know, your mom's over here for the book club," said Jeremy.

"Oh, yeah, well, I just have this silly question to ask her," Candace fibbed.

"Well, they're breaking for coffee," Jeremy told her. Then he had an idea. "Want to come over? We can hang out."

Candace put her hand over the receiver and screamed loudly.

Phineas and Ferb were outside signing for a delivery when they heard the piercing scream. "That was great, Ferb," Phineas said. "But you should really save those screams for

later, when the house is up and running." Ferb looked at Phineas blankly.

Candace was still in shock over the fact that Jeremy Johnson had just invited her over to his house! She tried to remain calm. "I mean, sure!" Candace told Jeremy, once she had recovered.

"Cool," he replied. "See you in about twenty minutes?"

But Jeremy didn't get a response. Candace had fainted on the kitchen floor!

Dr. Doofenshmirtz stood, along with several boxes of his belongings, next to a large purple jet. "Now, I'll just load up a few things that Professor Destructicon let me store here," he said. "If there's one thing Kevin understands, it's closet space." He smiled. "Now, I'll just, uh, grab my keys to the escape jet and, uh . . ." He stopped in midsentence and frantically patted his pockets. "Hmm . . . I

could've sworn I put them in my lab coat." He thought for a moment. "Oh, they're probably over here on the computer console." He walked over to look, but his keys weren't there, either. "No."

Perry looked down, and lo and behold, the keys were on a cute little doggy key chain, right near one of his webbed feet! Slowly and quietly, he stepped on the keys and slid them out of sight.

Dr. Doofenshmirtz walked by. "Ah! The kitchen!" he cried. "Hello? Keys?" But they weren't there. He leaned in close to Perry. "This is a *little* bit awkward," he admitted, "but have you seen my escape-jet keys?"

Perry nodded.

Dr. Doofenshmirtz was pleasantly surprised to hear this piece of news. "What, you have?" he said delightedly. "Well, that's great. Where are they?"

Perry closed his eyes and turned his head.

There was no way he was letting the evil doctor know that he was hiding his keys!

"You won't tell me?" cried Dr. Doofenshmirtz, his eyes wide with disbelief. "Is that because you don't speak, or are you just being a jerk?"

Twenty minutes was not a lot of time to come up with the perfect outfit. But Candace had to get to Jeremy's house soon! The floor of her room was littered with clothes—pants, shirts, skirts, dresses, shoes, and boots—pretty much the entire contents of her closet.

"I can't believe it!" she squealed. "I'm finally going to Jeremy's house!" She paused and took a deep breath. "Okay, now, what would the perfect look be?" She stood up, holding a T-shirt in front of her. Her back was to the window, so she didn't see Phineas cheerfully walking by with a guillotine, or Ferb passing by pushing a stretcher with a fake dead body on it.

Suddenly Candace had an idea. "I know!" she exclaimed. "Girl-next-door-meets-pop-diva-meets-Hollywood–bad girl, crossed with an old-school glamour goddess!"

This time, she missed her brothers carrying a suit of armor and a Frankenstein head in a jar. "Now," she said, "I've just got to find the finishing touch." She bent down to rummage through the giant pile of clothing.

Voila! She was finally done. She ran into the backyard dressed in a cropped T-shirt, jeans, and boots, with a scarf casually tossed

around her neck. Even her bicycle helmet matched her outfit.

"Hey, boys!" she called. "I'm off to the Johnsons' book club." She couldn't resist adding, "Jeremy invited me over." She smiled proudly.

Candace was so distracted that she didn't notice Ferb sharpening an ax or Phineas holding the jar with the Frankenstein head in it.

"Um, when you see Mom, could you tell her some snakes got lost in the house?" Phineas asked.

"Okay," she said with a big grin. She hadn't paid any attention to what her brother had just said. "You boys have fun! See ya!"

Chapter 3

Gathered in the backyard were a group of kids from the neighborhood. There were the Fireside Girls dressed in scout uniforms, Buford the town bully, and Phineas and Ferb's friend Baljeet. Ferb sat nearby on a box while Phineas stood and addressed the group.

"Okay, troops," he said. "Thanks for coming on such short notice. Buford, I know this is cutting into your canasta game."

Buford scowled. "This better be good, Pointy." He pounded his fist into his palm.

"Oh, it is," Phineas assured him. "Isabella has been cursed. . . ."

The kids all gasped in horror.

"With hiccups!" finished Phineas.

"Aw!" they wailed.

"Worst case I've ever seen," Phineas explained. "We're building this haunted house to scare the hiccups out of her. To do so, we must dig deep into those terrible places any sane man shoves into the darkest, most twisted corners of his mind. Each of you must find out what scares you the most." He looked over at the group, which seemed terrified. "As

you can see," he continued, "today we're building a haunted house, electronically controlled by this giant organ." He pointed to the large instrument. "Every room is monitored on these screens, and by playing the keys, I can trigger all sorts of surprises." To demonstrate, he hit a key and a ghost popped out of the box that Ferb had been sitting on. Ferb went flying through the air and into the haunted house! "So, with your help, my friends, we can build this house with enough horror to destroy the involuntary contraction of Isabella's diaphragm muscle once and for all!"

Ferb threw open the doors to the house and staggered out.

"Oh, there you are, Ferb," said Phineas. He turned back to the group. "Okay, people, let's get our scare on!"

Dr. Doofenshmirtz was still looking for his keys. He had resorted to playing the hot-or-cold game with Perry. "Am I getting warmer?" he asked the platypus. "Hmm?" When Perry wouldn't answer, he tried another tactic. "Ah-ha! The sofa! My keys fell between the cushions, right?" But still, no response from Perry. "Ah . . . no. Oh, come on! I defeated you fair and square, Perry the Platypus. Why can't you accept your death with dignity and maturity and play the game with me?" He walked back over to the secret agent. Perry scowled.

"Fine. Be that way," said Dr. Doofenshmirtz, crossing his arms. "I'll find my keys myself and teach you the meaning of grace under fire." Just then the Disintevaporator beeped. The countdown read 20:47, in big red numbers. Time was running out.

But to the evil scientist,

grace under fire apparently meant getting down on his hands and knees and begging. "Please, I'll do anything!" Dr. Doofenshmirtz cried. "Oh, for the love of great Caesar's ghost, what would you have me do?"

The time now read 10:39. Perry smiled. He had a plan. He decided to make the doctor balance on one foot, on top of a rubber ball, while spinning two plates.

It wasn't easy. "Aah! Aah!" the doctor cried.

* * *

As Candace rode her bike to Jeremy's house, she felt as if she were floating on a cloud of happiness. A rainbow unfurled its beautiful colors against the clear blue sky. Roses bloomed, birds chirped, and butterflies fluttered by. A flower seller standing in the middle of the street gave her a bouquet and kissed her hand.

Little did Candace know that Jeremy's sister, Suzy, and her tiny pet poodle were standing by the window, waiting for her to arrive. When Candace rode up to the house, the little dog bared its teeth. Suzy closed the blinds with an evil smile and opened the front door. Totally clueless as to  what awaited her, Candace took off her helmet and bent over to put it down. That's when the poodle ran out and bit her in the rear.

"Help, somebody!" Candace screamed. "Ooh, get it off me! These are designer jeans!" But the dog wouldn't let go. Frantically, Candace spun around to see Suzy turning on the lawn sprinklers. "Wait, what are you doing?" she cried. Whoosh! Candace's carefully arranged hair was suddenly dripping wet. "No! Wah! My hair! Help! He—"

Suddenly, Candace fell face-first into a pile of mud. She looked up and saw a remote-controlled car headed straight toward her. "Huh?" she said, puzzled.

Suzy giggled as she expertly controlled the car, causing it to back up and spin its wheels in the mud. Candace was now completely covered.

"Aah!" Candace wailed. "Why are you doing this to me?"

Suzy responded by laughing wickedly at Candace.

Just then, Jeremy poked his head out of the door. "Suzy?" he said. "What's going on out here?" Then he  spotted Candace lying in the muddy grass, with their poodle continuing to tear away at the seat of her pants. "Candace?" he asked in disbelief.

Candace smiled weakly. "Oh . . . uh, hi, Jeremy," she said. She tried to act casual, as if it were completely normal to be lying facedown in the mud on someone's front lawn with a small poodle attached to them.

Suzy turned to her brother. "Upsies," she said, reaching up. Jeremy bent down to pick up his little sister.

Candace was fuming. "Wait, no! Don't pick her up! She's evil! Evil!" She struggled to stand up and pointed at Suzy. "Can't you see? She's out to get me! She did this to me!"

"What are you talking about?" Jeremy said with a chuckle. "Little Suzy wouldn't hurt a fly."

Suzy giggled like an innocent toddler. "Bubble!" she cried.

Candace's eyes narrowed. "No! She's trying to get rid of me! Can't you see?" She put her hands to her head. "I can't take it!"

"Wait, Candace!" called Jeremy.

"No! If you can't see it, I should leave while I still have a shred of dignity left," Candace said. She picked up her helmet, which had the poodle attached to it, and put it on her head.

"Candace, come back!" shouted Jeremy. But Candace pedaled off.

Suzy couldn't have been happier. Her work here was done. She waved to Candace's retreating back. "Bye-bye," she said from her big brother's arms. No one is going to take Jeremy away from me, Suzy thought with satisfaction.

Chapter 4

Isabella headed into the backyard. "Hi, Phineas," she said. "Whatcha do . . . Ph-Phineas?" She hiccupped. A moment later, she noticed that she was standing in front of a large, scary haunted house, complete with screeching bats circling the roof. Isabella covered her face and screamed as they swooped down on her. Just then, a shadow loomed in front of her. She gasped and slowly began to

back away from a huge sluglike monster that was creeping toward her. It was huge and had glowing red eyes. Inside its gaping mouth were a green tongue and pointy teeth.

Even though the costume was really scary, Isabella knew it was Phineas in disguise. She let out another hiccup. "Darn," she said. "It didn't work, Phineas."

Phineas sighed. He unzipped his monster suit. Now he was wearing a mad-scientist outfit and a giant red and maroon wig.

"What else you got?" Isabella asked eagerly.

Phineas clasped his hands together. "Oh, we've got plenty," he said. "If you're up to it."

39

Isabella touched his yellow-gloved hand. "I—" Isabella hiccupped, "g-g-guess so."

Phineas led Isabella toward the haunted house. Ferb, dressed as Frankenstein, was playing eerie music on an organ. The front door opened with a creak, and Phineas and Isabella walked inside.

They saw one terrifying sight after another. The lights turned off, and when they came back on, the two friends were surrounded by hideous creatures. They ran through a room

filled with piles of bones and guarded by howling dogs with glowing green eyes. In the next room a series of ghosts jumped out at them. Phineas and Isabella held hands and raced up a circular stairway. At the top, a scary jack-in-the-box popped out. In the upstairs hallway the walls were covered with axes and other dangerous weapons. At the end of the hall, a coat of armor lowered a large ax, nearly slamming into them! They skidded to a stop, and then jumped over the ax together.

Then they ran into another room. There they found Baljeet dressed as a large piece of paper, with the word FAIL written on it.

"Boo! Boo! I say," Baljeet cried.

"Baljeet," Phineas said, greeting him. He knew it was just his friend in disguise.

Baljeet shook his head. "Oh, I am not Baljeet. I am the scariest thing known to man: a failed math test!" He waved his arms around spookily.

Phineas was not impressed. "Yeah, right," he commented. "We're just going to move on now." He and Isabella left the room.

Baljeet chased after them. "You can run, but it won't be to the college of your choice, I tell you!" he shouted.

Next, Phineas and Isabella encountered a big robot, a group of zombie witches with long green hair, a hallway full of spooky portraits, and dozens of creepy spiders falling from the ceiling. They continued to run through the house.

Then they came to a dark room. A figure stood in the corner with a little dog. The figure turned around as the curtains blew eerily. It looked like a little girl with pigtails. The dog dropped to its side, forgotten.

"Hello?" Phineas called. "Buford?"

"Behold: the face of evil," Buford announced.

Phineas couldn't believe his eyes. "Buford, are you supposed to be Jeremy's little sister?" he asked. "You said you were going to be something scary!"

"She *is* scary, man," Buford replied. "She gives me the willies."

Phineas and Isabella stared at Buford. "Little Suzy Johnson gives you the willies?" Phineas asked in disbelief.

Buford shook his head. "You don't know, man. You don't know!"

Phineas and Isabella slowly backed out of the room. "Uh . . . we'll catch up with you later, okay?"

Buford knelt on the ground, turned on a faucet, and began rubbing his hands together. "Wash away the horror. Wash away the horror," he chanted.

Outside the room, Phineas grabbed a rope, and he and Isabella were lifted into the air. Bats circled and screeched around them. At the top was a roller-coaster car with a skull on

it. They hopped into it, riding past grave-stones, spiders, monsters, and evil clowns. They came to a stop where they had begun, right behind where Ferb was playing the organ. Ferb turned around and let out an evil laugh.

Still sitting in the roller-coaster car, Phineas turned to his companion. "So, Isabella, did it work?"

In response, Isabella hiccupped.

"I was afraid she would say that," Phineas said to himself. "Well, there's one more thing we could try. . . ."

Candace huffed and puffed as she pedaled home, the crazy poodle still clinging to her helmet. Suddenly, she saw something that made her stop short.

The dog fell off her head and ran toward his home, whining with fear. Candace couldn't believe her eyes. "I don't believe this!" she cried.

She had just caught sight
of the giant haunted
house Phineas and Ferb
had built. And she was
not happy about it!

Back at the island, Dr. Doofenshmirtz was
still trying to figure out how to get his keys
away from Perry.

"Let me get this straight," he said. "If I set
you free, you'll give me the keys, right?"

Perry nodded.

"Oh, for Pete's sake!" cried Dr. Doofenshmirtz. "Why didn't you say that, like, an
hour ago?" He pressed a button on his remote
control, which released the restraints. Perry
lifted his foot, revealing the keys.

"Oh, look," said the evil scientist. "They
were under your cute little platypus foot the
whole time." Laughing maniacally, he grabbed
the keys and raced to the jet. "Open, open,

open," he pleaded, fumbling with the keys. Then he started loading the boxes filled with his belongings onto the jet. "Now, grab my stuff. Hurry. Hurry, hurry, must hurry." He jumped into the seat. "Seat belt and . . . ignition!" he cried. He pressed a button and the top lifted off the island.

Dr. Doofenshmirtz was out of breath. "Whew," he said, wiping his brow. "That was close." He sighed. "Now, let's just make sure I didn't forget anything in my haste." He turned around and started taking inventory. "Aah, got my old basketball, the lamp, Christmas lights, the umbrella, Perry the Platypus, the Disintevaporator, my golf—" Dr. Doofenshmirtz gasped. "*Perry the Platypus? The Disintevaporator? My golf clubs? I don't even play golf!*"

Perry launched himself forward and

attacked the evil scientist. Dr. Doofenshmirtz grabbed Perry and threw him across the jet. Then he jumped onto Perry. "How do you like it, huh?" he yelled. Perry tossed the evil scientist to the floor. Dr. Doofenshmirtz raised his hand and waved it. "Ah! Wait, wait, wait!" he cried. "Hold on. Time, time, time. I got a hair caught in my mouth. Ech! Ugh!" Then he grabbed the red and green Christmas lights from a box marked Xmas Stuff, spun them around like a lasso, and then tossed them so they wrapped around Perry.

Perry hit the hatch to the jet, and the lights wrapped around the lock and turned it. The hatch fell open, and Dr. Doofenshmirtz's stuff started getting sucked out of the jet.

"Ha-ha!" shouted Dr. Doofenshmirtz. "Since you saved me the trouble of opening the hatch,

let me show you out!" He returned to the controls and took a sharp left turn. All of the evil scientist's things went flying out. The lights spun out of the jet, and Perry went flying into the air as well. But at the last moment, he grabbed the string of lights, which were still attached to the jet, and hung on as if it were a rope.

Back at the haunted house, Candace was *really* angry. "Those two are in *such* big trouble," she said to herself.

But Phineas had one final plan to scare Isabella's hiccups away once and for all. "Okay, Ferb," he said, "raise the antenna." Ferb spun a wheel and a big, green, glowing lightning rod extended out of the roof. "Let's see if we

can up the scariness factor. You see, our haunted house is powered by static electricity. Maybe we can get a lightning strike to fire things up."

Candace walked inside the dark entryway of the haunted house. "Um, hello? Phineas? Ferb?" Her voice echoed eerily. "You two are in big trouble," she said uncertainly. The door suddenly slammed shut behind her. There was no way out. "Okay, you guys, stop fooling around! You guys better come out now. I'm getting really mad."

Suddenly, something darted behind Candace in the darkness. "What was that?" she cried. Just then, a huge monster jumped out of the shadows and opened its mouth. Out popped a smaller monster head, which opened to reveal an even smaller monster head, which opened to reveal the smallest monster head! Candace screamed, and her hair stood on end. She bolted out of the room.

After Candace had gone, three of the Fireside Girls lifted off their masks, giggling with delight that their trick had worked. "Yeah!" they cheered.

Candace found herself in a hallway with multiple closed doors. She opened one and heard a high-pitched scream. She screamed just as loudly. Back in the hallway, a ghostly floating candlestick followed her. "Stay away from me!" she shouted, ducking into another doorway. Candace now stood in the dark room, breathing hard. A pair of eyes shone in the darkness. Her hand trembling, Candace reached up and pulled a light switch. A vampire

was hanging upside down. "Good evening," he said pleasantly. "It *is* evening, isn't it?"

Candace ran out of the room, and bats circled around her. Dragon heads, dancing skeletons, a giant floating baby head, and Frankenstein's monster all appeared. And Candace could only think of one thing: PHINEAS!!!!

Chapter 5

Phineas stared at the static-electricity indicator. "Whoa, whoa, whoa!" he exclaimed. "Too much, Ferb. Too much! Look out!"

Candace had made it past the green monsters, a room filled with bones, and the hallway with the dozens of falling spiders. Next, she ran right into Buford, who was dressed as Suzy. Baljeet was right behind him. She couldn't believe her eyes when she saw

the bully dressed up as her archnemesis.

"Huh?" she cried, pointing at Buford. She screamed. So did Buford and Baljeet. Still screaming, she ran off through the jumping ghosts and past the wall of weapons, which were all launched at her. She sprinted up the stairs and then laid down on top of a trunk to rest. Suddenly, the trunk popped open, revealing the huge, ugly jack-in-the-box. Candace fell into the roller coaster, and it took off with her in it. Once the horrific ride was over, she was dumped unceremoniously at the feet of Phineas and Isabella.

"Candace?" said Phineas.

Candace lifted her head. She had fallen flat on the ground. She stood up and marched toward her brother. "Phineas, when Mom sees that you've built a haunted house in the backyard, with werewolves and vampires and a giant floating baby head . . ." She paused for a moment. "What's that even about?"

The giant floating baby head suddenly appeared and cooed.

"Not now!" Candace snapped. The giant floating baby head looked at her began to cry.

"And then there was a giant jack-in-the-box with a suit of armor that nearly took my head off!" Candace continued. "And you just drive me crazy!" She shook her head. "When I tell Mom what you're doing, you are going *down*! Down, down, down!" she shouted. The group just stared at her as she marched off.

Phineas turned to Isabella. "Is there any chance that *that* cured your hiccups?"

Isabella hiccupped again in response.

Candace marched over to the elevator of the haunted house and pressed the button. It opened, and she stepped inside. She turned around, and there was the giant floating baby head. Candace looked annoyed and lifted up her arms.

The baby head cooed again.

"Would you get out of here?" Candace said grumpily.

Crying, the baby head sadly got off the elevator.

Dr. Doofenshmirtz's escape jet flew through the air. Perry still trailed after it, clutching the string of Christmas lights. As they passed

Phineas and Ferb's haunted house, the end of the string of lights wrapped around the structure's lightning rod!

Candace heard her mom's car pull up in front of their house. She gasped with excitement. "Mom's home. Perfect!" she exclaimed. Now Phineas was really going to get it. There was no way he could explain away this one!

Her mom got out of the car with a bag of groceries and closed the door behind her.

Candace ran to the car. "Mom, Mom, Mom, Mom! Wait till you see what Phineas and Ferb have done!" she yelled.

As Buford and some of the other kids watched in disbelief, the jet started to pull the haunted house off its foundation. The Fireside Girls ran out of the house in a panic, followed by Ferb and Isabella. The house began to lift off the ground! Phineas poked his head

out of a gaping wall. "What's happening?" he cried. "Uh, guys? A little help!"

"Phineas!" cried Isabella.

"Aaaah!" shouted Phineas. He leaned forward, and the wall broke. He fell out of the house, tumbling toward the ground.

Isabella rallied the Fireside Girls. "Quick, everyone, sashes!" she ordered. The girls gathered their sashes, and with a snap, wove them together, forming a fireman's net, of sorts. The girls each held a corner. Phineas fell into the net, bounced in the air, and landed safely in Isabella's arms.

"Now, *that* was scary," said Isabella. Then she realized something. "Hey, my hiccups are gone!"

Ferb gave her a thumbs-up.

Candace had dragged her mom into the backyard. They watched as the Fireside Girls filed past them. "See?" said Candace. "Absolute terror. These little creeps have destroyed our backyard, leaving this ugly mess in its place." She pointed to the place where the haunted house *used* to be. But instead she was pointing at Baljeet. He waved.

"Hi, Baljeet," called Candace's mom. She looked disapprovingly at her daughter. "That wasn't very nice, Candace." Shaking her head, she turned and went inside.

* * *

Perry wound his way down the string of lights to the top of the haunted house, which was now flying through the air. Dr. Doofenshmirtz threw the Disintevaporator out of the plane and toward Perry. "There you go, Perry the Platypus!" the evil scientist shouted. "Enjoy your disintevaporation!" It hit the roof of the house with a bang, breaking the string of lights which had held it to the jet. Perry flew through the air, coolly snapping a belt around his waist and deploying a parachute.

The haunted house smashed to the ground right behind Candace. Aha! Candace thought. Now I've got them! She laughed in delight and

then ran to the house and threw open the door. "It's back! Mom, it's back!" she cried breathlessly.

And as the Disintevaporator counted down, five . . . four . . . three . . . two . . . one, the haunted house disappeared in a flash of light! Candace came out of the house, yanking her mother by the hand. "It's back! I told you! It's returned!" Her eyes on her mother, Candace pointed to where the house had been just a few seconds ago. But all her mom saw was Baljeet, holding his book bag.

"Oh, excuse me," he said. "I forgot my satchel."

Candace's mom had had enough. "Good-bye, Candace," she said with a sigh. She slammed the door shut.

Candace stood there, blinking in disbelief.

Isabella looked over at her. "What's the matter?" she asked.

"Phineas and Ferb are the matter," Candace complained. "This day was ruined, and I didn't even get to hang out with Jeremy."

Isabella gave her a sympathetic look. "Sorry, but you know, it was the best day for me! Due to my incurable case of the hiccups, I spent an entire day showered with undivided attention from Phineas. It was wonderful," she finished happily.

"Hiccups?" Candace said excitedly. She clasped her hands together and smiled.

"Hey, Candace," a voice said, "you ran away so quickly, we didn't get a chance to—" Candace turned around. It was Jeremy!

Candace said nothing. She merely . . . hiccupped.

Jeremy looked concerned. "Sounds like you got a bad case of the hiccups." He put his hand on her shoulder.

Candace hiccupped again.

"Here, come on," Jeremy said. "Let's see what we can do about that." He put his arm around her, and they walked off together. "I've got a glass of water with your name on it."

As they left, they passed Jeremy's sister, Suzy. Candace hissed at her.

"What? What did I do?" Suzy asked Buford innocently.

Buford chuckled nervously. "Um, I-I'll just, uh . . . go," he said.

Phineas and Ferb were relaxing in the backyard. Phineas was leaning against a tree trunk, his arms behind his head. Ferb was lying in the grass next to Perry.

"That was a great day, Ferb," Phineas said. "What do you think the scariest thing was?"

Ferb spoke for the first time that day. He didn't need to think twice. "Definitely the giant floating baby head," he said.

Phineas turned to him. "Yeah," he said in agreement. He thought for a minute. "Yeah, where did that *come* from?"

Ferb shrugged.

Phineas furrowed his brow. "Hmm," he wondered aloud.

Just then in the distance, he heard Isabella hiccup. "Darn," she said.

But Phineas just laughed to himself. Oh well, he thought. I guess we didn't cure Isabella's hiccups after all. But at least we had a blast trying!

Part Two

Chapter 1

Phineas and Ferb lived by one rule and one rule only: "Summer is short, you've got to make every day count!" And so the two step-brothers somehow managed to turn even the most boring day into an incredible adventure. Today, they stood in line at the Pharaoh Theater with Ferb's dad (who was also Phineas's stepdad) and Candace, Phineas's older sister (who was also Ferb's stepsister).

They were waiting to buy tickets to the classic mummy movie, *The Mummy with Two Tombs*. The theater was awesome—made up of a big golden sphinx, a temple complete with columns, and a giant pyramid.

As usual, Phineas was awaiting his and Ferb's next adventure, and Candace had a scowl on her face. She knew, she just *knew*, that her redheaded little brother was up to something. And Ferb, wearing his favorite pair of super–high-waisted pants, had their pet platypus, Perry, tucked under his arm. Ferb was Phineas's right-hand man and was ready

to assist in whatever way he could.

"You know, kids," their dad said as he purchased the tickets, "this theater was built over seventy years ago in this Neo-Egyptian style, and apparently there used to be a whole display of a pharaoh's tomb with a mummy in his sarcophagus." They headed into the theater, filing past a *Bones of Doom* movie poster picturing a flaming skull. "I mean, you couldn't pick a better place to watch a classic old mummy movie."

Phineas grinned at Ferb. A mummy in a

tomb made out of stone? Things were starting to get interesting!

They settled into their seats, and the movie began. *The Mummy with Two Tombs* was an old black-and-white film. As they watched, a short archaeologist with a rather large black mustache and a helmet held a flaming torch up to an inscription carved in stone. Nearby stood an ancient mummy, its arms crossed, inside a stone tomb covered in cobwebs. His fellow archaeologist, who was tall and thin, leaned over the shorter one's shoulder to see the hieroglyphics.

"There's an inscription here," the short archaeologist said. "An incantation of some sort." He began to read it aloud: *"Oh, wah ta goo siam."* Unbeknownst to the two men, the mummy's bloodshot eyes snapped open.

In the audience, Phineas's and Ferb's eyes widened in surprise.

Phineas turned to his father. "Dad, where

do you find a mummy?" he asked eagerly.

"Hidden deep in the bowels of the pyramids," his dad whispered. Just then, his cell phone rang. "Whoops. Better put this on vibrate."

Onscreen, the short archaeologist explained to his companion, "The incantation will make the mummy come to life and obey your commands!" He put his finger to his lips, deep in thought. He didn't realize that his partner was already inside the coffin with his arms folded across his chest, just like a mummy. He *also* didn't know that the mummy was standing behind him with its arms raised in a very

menacing way. The mummy reached down, about to grab his helmet. It was alive!

"Well, beat me with a chicken!" the short archaeologist exclaimed.

Obeying his command, the mummy proceeded to beat him about the head and shoulders with a live chicken!

"Ow!" cried the archaeologist. "What? Ooh! Hey! Stop! It's a— Ooh! Hey!"

"Cool," Phineas said. "Dad, is it hard to get into a pyramid?" he asked.

"Yes, indeed," his dad answered. "Often you had to negotiate various booby traps that were set centuries before." He and Phineas both turned their attention back to the screen.

The mummy had just stepped on a large button on the tomb floor. "You ridiculous mummy!" cried the archaeologist. "You've just tripped one of your own booby traps!" Instantly, rocks began to fall from above, and

water poured out of the eyes of the stone bull sculptures in the tomb.

They took off, running past enormous columns, which began to crumble and fall. "She's going to blow!" the archaeologist shouted. "Whoa!" Just as they reached the entrance to the tomb, there was an enormous explosion. The mummy and the archaeologist leaped to safety. They made it—but just barely.

"Awesome booby trap!" Phineas cried. He turned to his brother. "Ferb, we should get our own mummy."

He began to daydream about how much better life would be if he and Ferb had an ancient Egyptian mummy to pal around with. There were so many cool things they could do together—like sharing a strawberry shake at the ice-cream parlor; lying in the grass and watching the clouds float by; helping the mummy knit the world's longest

scarf; swinging at the playground; doing simultaneous flips off the diving board at the town pool; going for long walks on the beach; scaring away Buford the bully; always having a handkerchief for you when you needed one; playing checkers; going fishing; riding bikes; showing off to the kids at school—no one else would have a three-thousand-year-old mummy, that was for sure. The possibilities were endless!

"That would be awesome!" Phineas exclaimed. He turned to his father. "Dad, can we—"

But his father was sound asleep. He began to snore loudly.

"Come on, Ferb," Phineas said. "We'll be back before he wakes up." The two brothers took off running. They were going on a mummy hunt!

Chapter 2

Candace's eyes narrowed as she watched the boys head out of the theater. They were always getting into some sort of trouble. Well, this time things were going to be different. "Oh . . . those bozos aren't pulling anything on my watch," she said. She climbed over her father, who was still fast asleep.

Phineas, Ferb, and Perry walked up the aisle, through the swinging doors, and out into the theater lobby, almost knocking over a large bubble-gum machine. Candace was right behind them. Unfortunately, her head got caught between the swinging doors. Ouch!

"Hey, Ferb. Where's Perry?" Phineas asked. It was so weird. The platypus was there just seconds ago!

What the brothers didn't know was that Ferb's unassuming pet was actually a government secret agent for the OWCA (Organization Without a Cool Anagram). Perry had one mission: to foil the evil scientist Dr. Heinrich Doofenshmirtz and his elaborate, though inept, plans for world domination. Wearing his trademark secret-agent hat, Perry stood in front of a large plastic ape display for a movie called *Big Ape*. The ape's stomach opened, and Perry quickly jumped inside and straight into an open car, which began

speeding down a track. A white-haired man with a mustache appeared on the car's video screen. It was Major Monogram.

"Morning," said the major. He got right down to business. "Agent P, Doofenshmirtz is at it again," he reported. "It appears that he's purchased a string of odd items." He began reading from a piece of paper in his hand. "One pound of blood sausage—" He stopped reading and put his hand to his mouth, looking embarrassed. "Eh, that's my grocery list." He pulled out another sheet of paper. "Here it is. One magnet, one map of the city's drainage pipes, and two tons of scrap metal." Perry listened carefully and took notes. "It's in your hands now, Agent P," he said, pointing to Perry. "Over and out!"

The communication complete, the car Perry was riding in reached the end of the

track and flew into the air. Perry expertly flipped out of it and landed behind the controls inside a submarine. There were three buttons on the dashboard—DIVE, DON'T DIVE, and DESCEND. Perry chose DIVE. The top of the submarine banged shut. "Dive, dive, dive," the submarine computer droned. But the vehicle immediately hit bottom, only halfway underwater. Apparently, the water wasn't too deep. With a loud scraping noise, it dragged across the floor.

79

Back in the theater lobby, Phineas approached a young man wearing what looked like authentic ancient Egyptian dress—sandals, a loincloth, a headdress, and wrist cuffs. There was a name tag stuck to his chest.

"Mister employee, sir, where's the mummy exhibit?" Phineas asked politely.

The employee reached over and pushed the button on the wall intercom. "Manager assistance requested," he said in a bored tone.

An older man dressed in a similar costume

walked over to them. "Yes?" he asked.

"These boys want to know where the mummy exhibit is," the other employee said.

"It's in storage," replied the manager. "In the basement." He walked off.

Phineas grinned. Now they were getting somewhere! "Guess who's going to the basement!" he exclaimed, rushing off. Ferb followed right behind him.

A woman wearing purple cat's-eye glasses approached the young employee. "Uh, excuse me," she said. "Where are the restrooms?"

He pressed the intercom again. "Manager assistance requested," he repeated.

The manager appeared again. "Yes?" he said. Now that the employees were distracted, Phineas and Ferb were in the clear!

Meanwhile, Candace, who was crouched down behind some plants in the lobby, had been spying on her brothers. She pushed the

leaves aside to get a better look as they entered through a door marked STAIRWELL.

"There they go!" Candace muttered between gritted teeth. She *knew* they had been planning another one of their crazy schemes. She just knew it! And this time, they were *not* going to get away with it!

Chapter 3

Phineas and Ferb found themselves in a dusty room. Inside were a janitor's bucket, old boxes, and some Egyptian objects, including a large SEE THE MUMMY sign on the wall. Phineas spotted an old box filled with explorers' gear.

"Look! Pith helmets!" he said excitedly. "We must be going the right way! Say something pithy!" The brothers each grabbed

a helmet, blew off the dust, and put them on their heads.

Back in the lobby, Candace was seething with anger. "That's it!" she shouted. "I'm calling Dad!" She sat down on the carpet and pulled out a pink cell phone. She punched in her father's number and waited for him to answer. But he was still sleeping soundly, and his phone was on vibrate. The phone buzzed away in Mr. Flynn's pocket, tickling him. He giggled and shifted position, curling up in the theater chair. "Ahh," he said, falling back asleep.

When Candace didn't get an answer, she snapped her phone shut. "Oh, forget it," she said disgustedly. "I'm going in myself." She ran for the door that her brothers had just walked through. On the way in, she knocked into the velvet ropes, and their stands went down like a row of dominoes. The last one hit

the gigantic bubble-gum machine. The glass top, filled with multicolored gum balls, fell off its base, and landed on the lobby floor with a loud crash.

Candace ran through the door and stepped right into the janitor's bucket. She then proceeded to bounce down the stairs. "Aaah!" she screamed.

Phineas and Ferb opened the door on the landing. "Did you hear that?" asked Phineas. "Maybe it's the mummy!" he added hopefully.

Candace came to a crashing stop at the bottom of the stairs. She looked down at her

soggy feet and winced. "Ew!" she groaned. "My shoe is all squishy!"

Back in the lobby, the top of the bubble-gum machine rolled across the floor and through the doorway. It began to bounce down the stairs. Phineas and Ferb heard the noise and turned to see the big glass ball heading right toward them! They took off running down the stairs as fast as they could. At the bottom, they ran down a hallway, the top of the gum-ball machine in hot pursuit. To Phineas's shock, Ferb swung himself up and jumped onto Phineas' shoulders.

"Uh . . . Ferb?" said Phineas. "What are you doing?"

Ferb grabbed a pipe and expertly swung himself and his brother through the air. They did a flip and landed on top of the gumball machine. "Whoa!" cried Phineas.

Phineas was having a great time during this latest adventure. "Who knew looking for

mummies would be so much fun!" he exclaimed. "Watch this!" He did a handstand on the ball. Ferb quickly sat on the ball and  then jumped back up. They took off their helmets and started doing a dance as the ball rolled faster and faster. And then the ball rolled through a low entryway, and Phineas and Ferb's fun ride came to a sudden end. They hit the wall with a bang. Miraculously, when they landed on the hard floor, their hats wound up right in place on their heads.

"Hey, Ferb!" cried Phineas, sitting on the floor. "This was our first booby trap!" They gave each other a high-five. "Whoo!" This day was turning out even better than they had expected. Suddenly, Phineas spotted what they had been searching for. He pointed to a nearby door. "Hey, look! Storage! We're here!" he exclaimed.

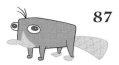

Meanwhile, Candace was getting more and more frustrated with her brothers. "Ohh!" she groaned. "When I catch them . . ." Suddenly she gasped. The giant bubble-gum-filled ball was rolling toward her! She screamed and grabbed an overhead pipe so she could swing herself out of its path. But that trick didn't work as well for her as it had for Ferb. The pipe came right off in her hands! She tossed it to the side and reached up, managing to grab another pipe. This time she was able to flip herself up into the vent. Crash! Bang! Boom! When she emerged from the other end, her hair was tousled, she had a bump on her head, and her clothes were ripped and stained. And the ball was still right behind her! "Oh, give me a break!" she screeched.

Frantically, she turned the

corner, running as fast as she could. To her surprise, the ball suddenly moved ahead of her. She watched it roll away, then she walked off in the other direction. Whew, she thought. That was close!

The ball bounced up the handrail to a set of stairs, then bounced onto a landing in front of an elevator door. It rolled forward, hit the elevator button, rolled back, and hit the handrail. The timing was perfect—the ball shot right into the open elevator doors. The doors closed behind it.

Candace spotted the elevator. She was anxious to get back inside the theater, where she could watch the rest of the movie and be safe. She hit the elevator button, and the doors opened. She stepped inside, the doors closing behind her. She faced forward, and then realized she was sharing the elevator with the giant ball! She screamed and ran out before the doors closed, the ball still right behind her.

She raced down one flight of stairs, jumping down the last few to the landing, and then hurtled down another set of stairs. The ball was still chasing her—it bounced on the landing and headed down the next flight of stairs. At the bottom of the steps Candace ran straight down a hallway. Suddenly the ball shattered, scattering small, colorful, round objects everywhere!

Candace ducked into a door marked SUPPLIES and plopped down on the floor to rest. What were those strange round objects all over the floor? she wondered. She reached forward, picked one up, then popped it into her mouth.

It was sweet with a candy coating. And it was very, very sticky. "Bubble gum?" she said in disbelief as she tried to pry her teeth apart. But they were stuck firmly together. "Oh, really old, stale bubble gum!" she realized. "Blech . . ."

Candace reached out to pull herself up and grabbed onto a nearby storage shelf. It started to shake. A tin of popcorn butter fell from the top shelf, drenching her. Then a large cardboard box opened up, and rolls of toilet paper fell down on her, sticking to the butter and wrapping around her body. The empty box fell on her head, and she stumbled forward blindly, her arms outstretched. She looked just like a mummy.

This was terrible! And there was only one

person to blame. One person who had gotten her into this ridiculous mess . . .

"Phineas!" she bellowed through a mouthful of bubble gum.

Chapter 4

It was, at first glance, a beautiful scene. Crystal clear waters surrounded by rolling green hills. Several beavers busily building a dam. Snowcapped mountains in the distance. Above it all a cloudless blue sky . . .

And a large metal machine smack-dab in the middle! Dr. Doofenshmirtz hummed to himself as he painted red letters on the side of his latest devious invention. "Almost done!"

he cried. "Just one more little bit."

To Dr. Doofenshmirtz's surprise, Perry flew through the air and knocked the paintbrush out of his hand with a roundhouse kick. The brush rolled across the platform, leaving a trail of red paint.

"Perry the Platypus," Dr. Doofenshmirtz said with a smirk. "As usual, your timing is *incredible*." He rubbed his hands together. "And by incredible, of course, I mean . . ." He mumbled something unintelligible. But Perry wasn't listening anyway. He was already planning his next move.

The two faced off. Dr. Doofenshmirtz pulled out a ray gun and shot it at Perry. The platypus was instantly enveloped by a thick bubble. He struggled to escape, jumping up and down and punching at its sides.

"No use, Perry the Platypus," said Dr. Doofenshmirtz. "I made this out of something

that can't be penetrated—*pure evil*! And a blend of space-age polymers," he added.

The doctor began to explain his scheme, which, as usual, was a strange one. "You see, Perry the Platypus, I'm going to unleash the water being held by this dam into that huge drainage pipe that leads directly to the ocean. The additional water will raise the sea level by two percent and then my property one block from the shoreline will become beachfront property." He laughed and ripped off his lab coat to reveal that he was wearing water wings and a bathing suit. He pumped his fists in excitement and put his lab coat back on.

Dr. Doofenshmirtz continued telling Perry

all about his scheme. "And to release the water from the dam, I have invented a ray which attracts wood the way a magnet attracts metal! The Woodenator! Which was almost complete until you rudely interrupted me." He reached for something. "Oh, look at this, Perry, it's my paintbrush. You know, the one you knocked out of my hand a few moments ago." He drew a pair of glasses and a curly mustache on the bubble, directly over Perry's face. "Maybe you want to try to take it back from me now? Huh, you want to try? Ha-ha-ha. Good-bye, Perry the Platypus." He pushed the bubble off the platform with both

hands, and it bounced away over the water with Perry still trapped inside!

Back at the theater, Phineas and Ferb pushed open the storage-room door. The room was filled with movie displays—shark heads, UFOs, Roman columns . . . and right next to a large green dinosaur, an open tomb with a mummy inside. Bingo!

Phineas chanted the same words that he had heard the archaeologist say in the movie: *"Oh, wah tah goo siam."* He looked expectantly at the mummy. Nothing. He grabbed it by the legs and pulled it out of the tomb. It quickly deflated. It was just a fake, blow-up mummy. Phineas and Ferb were very disappointed.

Phineas scowled. "There's nothing down here but fake, promotional lobby junk," he said in disappointment. He headed toward the door.

He was about to say something to Ferb

when Candace, still wrapped up like a mummy, appeared in the doorway. "For all we know," Phineas continued, "there might not even *be* such a thing as a mummy." Ferb pointed to the mummy, which was waving its arms at Phineas. "Yeah, I'll be right with you," Phineas said dismissively.

"Phineas," Candace groaned.

Phineas gasped when he finally realized what was in front of him. The mummy had come alive and was standing with its arms outstretched! Phineas slammed the door shut and took off—running right into Ferb. They

both screamed and jumped up, their hats flying off their heads. Candace threw open the door and took off right behind them.

Trying to escape, Phineas and Ferb jumped into the open mouth of a shark display. The shark fell over. Their legs entangled, the brothers  crab-walked to a *Safari Man 2 in 2-D* display. Wearing their helmets, the brothers blended in perfectly with the explorer theme. But Candace, who was still wrapped in toilet paper and couldn't really see where she was going, ran right past them and straight into a movie poster of a huge bus.

"Phineas!" Candace yelled.

"Aah!" Phineas screamed. "Wow!" he exclaimed. "I didn't expect him to be so scary!

I mean, can you imagine the angry, twisted soul hidden under those bandages?"

"Phineas!" Candace howled as she ran by the display.

"Makes me shudder," Phineas admitted. He thought for a moment. "But you know what? We came down here looking for a mummy, and I'm not leaving without one! Let's get him!"

The chase began. First, Phineas grabbed the mummy, and Ferb managed to get a net over its head. Then, they were both able to jump on top of the mummy.

But before they knew it, the mummy was

somehow standing on their heads! Phineas and Ferb took off in opposite directions, and the mummy crashed to the floor. They ran and grabbed the empty coffin. Phineas took one side and Ferb grabbed the other. They surrounded the mummy and slammed the coffin shut. Mission accomplished!

Phineas was thrilled. "Hey, Ferb. We got our own mummy!" he cheered. The brothers high-fived. There was just one thing: "Now how are we going to get it home?" Phineas asked.

Chapter 5

"And . . . finished!" proclaimed Dr. Doofenshmirtz as he finished painting the *R* on the side of his latest invention, the Woodenator. He hit the START button. It beeped, and the large magnet began to glow, emitting a powerful charge that was headed directly toward the beaver

dam. Sticks were pulled from the dam and onto the magnet.

The beavers ran off, running right past Perry, who was still stuck in the bubble. One

of the beavers stopped and looked at Perry curiously. Perry chattered at him, and the beaver chattered back. The beaver picked up a nearby log and expertly gnawed it down to a toothpick. He rubbed it against his two giant front

teeth, then threw it over his shoulder. Then he chomped down on the bubble, which burst open. Perry was free! The two creatures shook hands, slapped tails, and ran off in opposite directions.

"It is working!" Dr. Doofenshmirtz exclaimed with an evil laugh. "It is functioning properly!" But then the doctor heard a noise behind him and spun around. There stood Perry, his hands on his hips.

"Perry the Platypus!" Dr. Doofenshmirtz yelled in surprise. "You defeated my bubble of pure evil? Ooh!"

He reached into his lab coat, pulled out his ray gun, and aimed another bubble at Perry. The platypus avoided it by leaping onto the platform where the doctor was standing. The giant bubble got jammed in the mouth of the drainage pipe. Perry grabbed the gun and it went off, trapping the two mortal enemies in the same bubble! They floated into the

103

air, landing in the water behind the dam. Just then the dam broke! Perry and Dr. Doofenshmirtz were directly in the path of a rushing torrent of water. Perry reached up, grabbed Dr. Doofenshmirtz's nose, and broke the bubble.

"Oh, no!" Dr. Doofenshmirtz exclaimed. "What? Is my nose really that pointy?" Then he screamed as he was swept up by the raging water. Perry managed to outrace it by running into a large pipe, which connected to a vast system of other pipes underneath the city. Some-how, Perry emerged in the subbasement of the Pharaoh Theater! He knew he didn't

have a moment to lose. As he raced down the hallway, the water thundered after him.

Back in the theater, Phineas and Ferb heard a loud rumbling. They had placed the coffin on wheels and were ready to take it home. Suddenly they were surrounded by water! They hopped up on top of the coffin and rode the waves.

"You know what this is," Phineas said delightedly. "Our second booby trap!" He

turned around and spotted Perry on the coffin, sailing right behind them.

"There you are, Perry," said Phineas.

The trio rode the waves, paddling away. "Whoo!" Phineas cheered. "Oh, yeah!" This was awesome! It was like a ride at an amusement park. The brothers raised their arms in the air. "Whoo!"

The next thing they knew, the water pressure built up so much that they shot out of the top of the head of the sphinx like a geyser. They rocketed across the street, landing on the opposite sidewalk. Phineas, Ferb, Perry,

and Candace sat on the ground, surrounded by wooden splinters from the coffin and strips of toilet paper.

"Hey, Candace," Phineas said to his sister. "You missed all the fun. Allow me to introduce our mummy." He turned, but the

mummy was nowhere to be seen. "Hey, where's our mummy?" he asked disappointedly. "Mummy? Mummy?"

Just then, their dad walked up to them. "Mummy has supper waiting for us at home," he said. He took a closer look at his daughter. "Candace, why are you all wet?"

Candace growled angrily. Phineas and Ferb had done it again!

In the car on the way home, Candace, Phineas, and Ferb sat together in the back-seat. Perry lay sprawled across Candace's lap, fast asleep.

Ferb spoke for the first time all day. "You know," he said, "mummies have their brains pulled out through their noses."

Candace sighed. "The lucky ones," she grumbled.

Don't miss the fun in the next
Phineas & Ferb book. . . .

Big-Top Bonanza

Adapted by N. B. Grace
Based on the series created by Dan Povenmire & Jeff "Swampy" Marsh

When Phineas and Ferb find out that Cirque du Lune is coming to town, they can't wait to see it. But when the show is cancelled, they decide to put on their very own circus. With Phineas as the ringmaster, and performances like mud-diving and hoop-jumping, soon they're bringing the house down! But when Candace tries to prove her brothers aren't just clowning around, will the show go on? Plus, when Phineas and Ferb decide to do absolutely nothing for a day, Candace is determined to prove that her brothers are up to something!